Dear Parents:

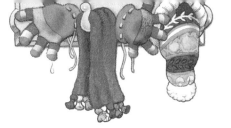

Congratulations! Your child is taking the first steps on an exciting journey. The destination? Independent reading!

STEP INTO READING® will help your child get there. The program offers five steps to reading success. Each step includes fun stories and colorful art or photographs. In addition to original fiction and books with favorite characters, there are Step into Reading Non-Fiction Readers, Phonics Readers and Boxed Sets, Sticker Readers, and Comic Readers—a complete literacy program with something to interest every child.

Learning to Read, Step by Step!

Ready to Read Preschool–Kindergarten
• big type and easy words • rhyme and rhythm • picture clues
For children who know the alphabet and are eager to begin reading.

Reading with Help Preschool–Grade 1
• basic vocabulary • short sentences • simple stories
For children who recognize familiar words and sound out new words with help.

Reading on Your Own Grades 1–3
• engaging characters • easy-to-follow plots • popular topics
For children who are ready to read on their own.

Reading Paragraphs Grades 2–3
• challenging vocabulary • short paragraphs • exciting stories
For newly independent readers who read simple sentences with confidence.

Ready for Chapters Grades 2–4
• chapters • longer paragraphs • full-color art
For children who want to take the plunge into chapter books but still like colorful pictures.

STEP INTO READING® is designed to give every child a successful reading experience. The grade levels are only guides; children will progress through the steps at their own speed, developing confidence in their reading. The F&P Text Level on the back cover serves as another tool to help you choose the right book for your child.

Remember, a lifetime love of reading starts with a single step!

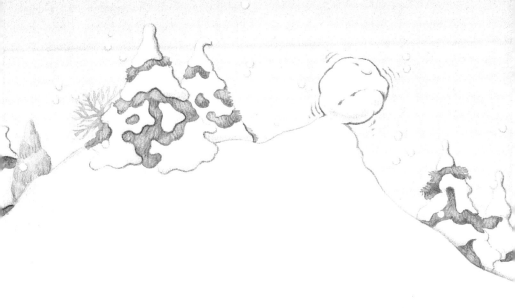

All rights reserved. Published in the United States by Random House Children's Books,
a division of Penguin Random House LLC, New York.

Step into Reading, Random House, and the Random House colophon are registered trademarks
of Penguin Random House LLC.

Visit us on the Web!
StepIntoReading.com
randomhousekids.com

Educators and librarians, for a variety of teaching tools, visit us at
RHTeachersLibrarians.com

Library of Congress Cataloging-in-Publication Data
Armstrong, Jennifer.
The snowball / by Jennifer Armstrong ; illustrated by Jean Pidgeon.
 p. cm. — (Step into reading. A step 1 book)
Summary: A small snowball gets bumped by a skier and rolls down the hill, growing in size
and picking up people as it goes.
ISBN 978-0-679-86444-8 (trade) — ISBN 978-0-679-96444-5 (lib. bdg.)
[1. Snow—Fiction. 2. Stories in rhyme.]
I. Pidgeon, Jean, ill. II. Title. III. Series: Step into reading. Step 1 book.
PZ8.3.A63 Sn 2003 [E]—dc21 2002013782

Printed in the United States of America 28 27 26 25 24 23 22 21 20 19

This book has been officially leveled by using the F&P Text Level Gradient™ Leveling System.

Random House Children's Books supports the First Amendment and celebrates the right to read.

THE SNOWBALL

by Jennifer Armstrong

illustrated by Jean Pidgeon

Random House New York

I saw a snowball

on a hill.

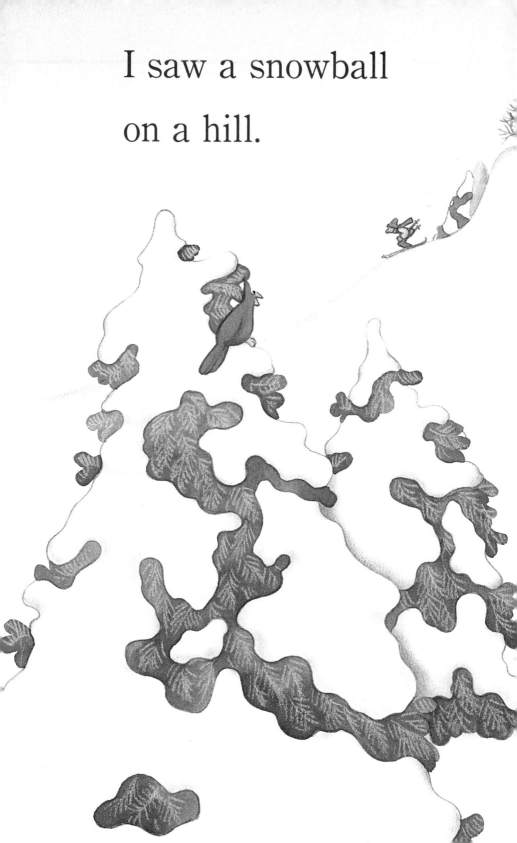

It rolled along
and picked up Bill!

It rolled along
with Bill inside.

It rolled along
and picked up Clyde.

What a ride!

I saw a snowball
with four feet.

It rolled along
and picked up Pete.

It rolled him up
as quick as that!

It rolled along
and picked up Pat.

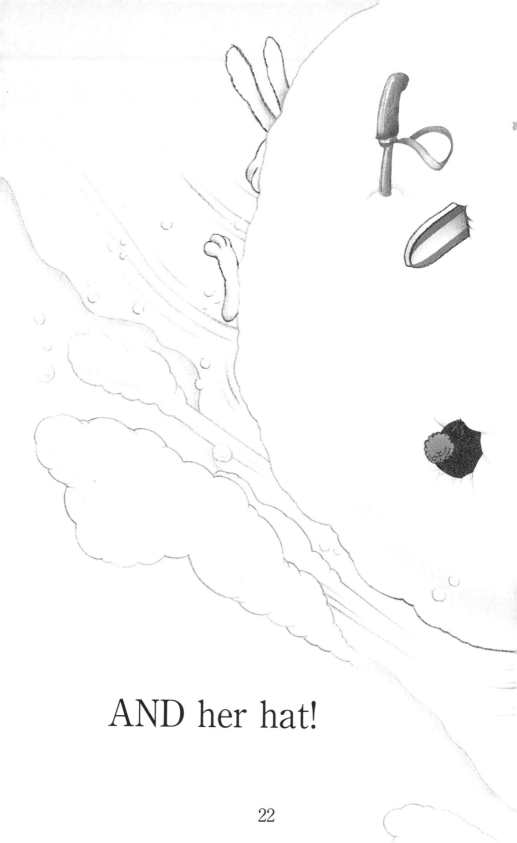

AND her hat!

I saw a snowball
roll past Lee.

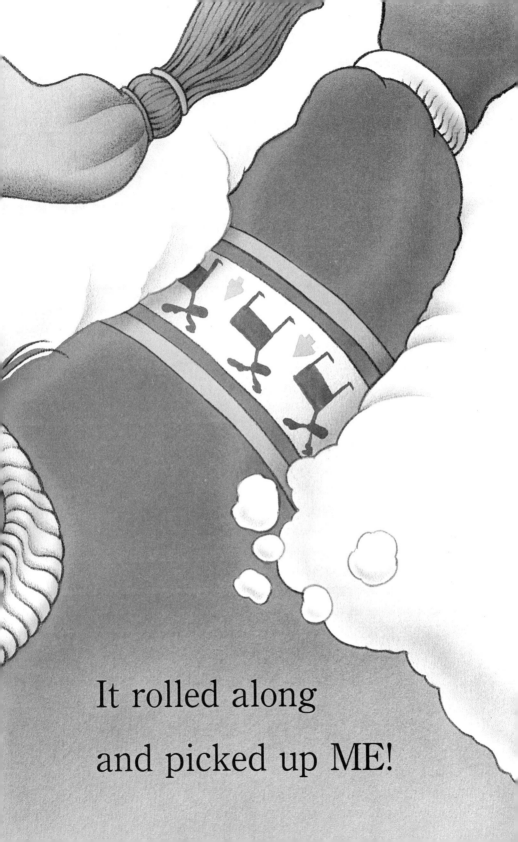

It rolled along
and picked up ME!

It rolled! It bounced!

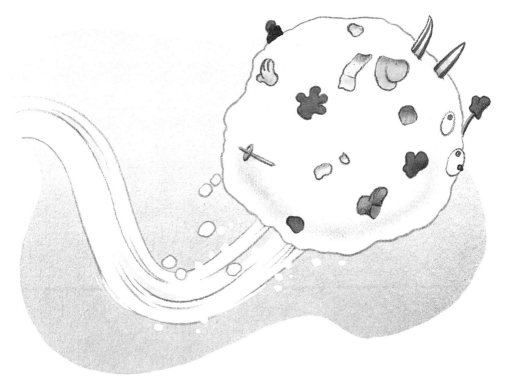

It dipped! It dashed!

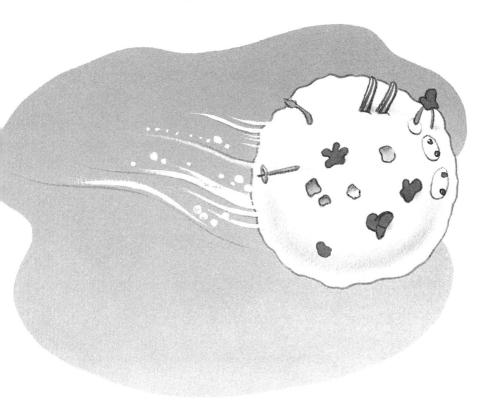

It rolled along
until it SMASHED!

THE END

31901060164748